FRANKiE SPARKS
AND THE CLASS PET

ALSO BY
MEGAN FRAZER BLAKEMORE

Frankie Sparks and the Talent Show Trick

FRANKIE SPARKS, THIRD-GRADE INVENTOR

FRANKIE SPARKS AND THE CLASS PET

BOOK 1

BY MEGAN FRAZER BLAKEMORE

ILLUSTRATED BY NADJA SARELL

ALADDIN   NEW YORK LONDON TORONTO SYDNEY NEW DELHI

This book is a work of fiction. Any references to historical events, real people, or real places are used fictitiously. Other names, characters, places, and events are products of the author's imagination, and any resemblance to actual events or places or persons, living or dead, is entirely coincidental.

❦ ALADDIN

An imprint of Simon & Schuster Children's Publishing Division
1230 Avenue of the Americas, New York, New York 10020
First Aladdin paperback edition June 2019
Text copyright © 2019 by Megan Frazer Blakemore
Illustrations copyright © 2019 by Nadja Sarell
Also available in an Aladdin hardcover edition.
All rights reserved, including the right of reproduction in whole or in part in any form.
ALADDIN and related logo are registered trademarks of Simon & Schuster, Inc.
For information about special discounts for bulk purchases, please
contact Simon & Schuster Special Sales at 1-866-506-1949 or
business@simonandschuster.com.
The Simon & Schuster Speakers Bureau can bring authors to your live event.
For more information or to book an event contact the Simon & Schuster Speakers
Bureau at 1-866-248-3049 or visit our website at www.simonspeakers.com.
Series art directed by Laura Lyn DiSiena
Interior designed by Tiara Iandiorio
The illustrations for this book were rendered in pencil line
on paper and digital flat tones.
The text of this book was set in Nunito.
Manufactured in the United States of America 0620 OFF
10 9 8 7 6 5 4
Library of Congress Cataloging-in-Publication Data
Names: Blakemore, Megan Frazer, author. | Sarell, Nadja, illustrator. | Title: Frankie Sparks and the class pet / by Megan Frazer Blakemore ; illustrated by Nadja Sarell. | Description: First Aladdin paperback edition. | New York : Aladdin, 2019. | Series: Frankie Sparks, 3rd grade inventor ; [1] | Summary: Frankie Sparks, the self-proclaimed "best inventor in the third grade," does research and creates a tool to try to persuade her classmates that a rat would make the best class pet.
Identifiers: LCCN 2018033416 (print) | LCCN 2018038819 (eBook) |
ISBN 9781534430457 (eBook) | ISBN 9781534430433 (pbk) |
ISBN 9781534430440 (hc)
Subjects: | CYAC: Schools—Fiction. | Pets—Fiction. | Inventions—Fiction.
Classification: LCC PZ7.B574 (eBook) | LCC PZ7.B574 Fm 2019 (print) |
DDC [Fic]—dc23
LC record available at https://lccn.loc.gov/2018033416

For my Dyer Dragons friends

CONTENTS

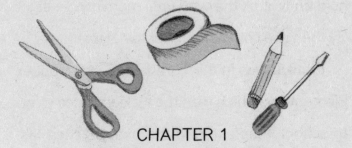

CHAPTER 1

The Big Announcement

FRANKIE SPARKS HAD A STORY TO share. It was the best story ever. It gurgled in her stomach as she rode the bus to school. It fizzed in her fingers and toes when she and Suki Moskovitz and Maya played Don't Touch the Hot Lava on the playground before school. It threatened to pop out of her mouth like a burp while they put their things away in their cubbies and did their morning work. But she managed to hold on to it all the way until morning meeting. By then she could barely contain herself.

Frankie was in third grade at Grace Hopper Elementary, which was the luckiest place to go to school. Plus she had the best teacher, Ms. Cupid. And her best friend in the whole world, Maya, was in her class, and Ms. Cupid even let them be partners 50 percent of the time.

Every Monday at morning meeting Ms. Cupid asked her class to share what they had done over the weekend. So, as soon as Frankie and her twenty classmates crowded down on the rug, Frankie raised her hand as high as she could. She stretched up on her knees and wiggled her fingers. But she didn't say anything. Not one word. Her teacher, Ms. Cupid, did not like it when kids blurted.

Ms. Cupid called on Lila Jones, who played with her shoelaces while she launched into a long story about her soccer game and how it had rained and how they had sat in their cars until the rain ended. Then they got to play the game, and Lila claimed they had won 3–2, but then Suki, who was on the team too, said, no, they had tied 3–3. *How could you not even know if you had won or tied the game?* Frankie wondered.

"What matters is that you both played very hard, I'm sure," Ms. Cupid said. "And were good sports about it."

Frankie thought that of course it mattered that they had played hard and were good sports, but it also mattered who had won or lost. It was a game, after all. "You really can't remember if you won or tied?" she asked.

"Frankie," Ms. Cupid warned. "We're moving on."

So Frankie shot her hand up into the air again. Ms. Cupid called on Luke Winslow, who talked about *his* soccer game. At least he knew who'd won—the other team—but he still went on and on and on.

When Luke was done, Frankie shot her hand into the air again, and finally Ms. Cupid called on her.

"We went to see my aunt at the university where she works. She's a rodentologist. And—"

"Excuse me, Frankie. I'm sorry to interrupt, but I think some of our friends might not know what a rodentologist is."

"It's someone who studies rodents. We got to see mice and hamsters and white rats and . . ." Frankie took a deep breath. This was the best part of her story. "A capybara." She pronounced the word slowly, just the way her aunt had taught her: *cap-ah-bear-ah.*

"It's like a guinea pig, but it's four feet long!" Frankie rocked forward. "I got to lie down next to it. It was longer than me!"

Capybara
Hydrochaerus hydrochaeris

"Cool!" Luke exclaimed.

Lila wrinkled her nose, but Suki said, "Wow!" Suki almost never said "Wow!" It was usually reserved for things like back hand-springs and T-shirts with glitter on them.

And of course Maya, Frankie's best friend in the whole wide world, gave Frankie a big grin.

"That is so cool, Frankie," Ms. Cupid agreed. And then she flipped over the page with the morning message on it and wrote down the word "rodentologist" on the blank piece of chart paper below. She tapped her pointer against the word. "What a great vocabulary word." Underneath it she wrote, *Biologist.* She explained, "A biologist is some-one who studies living things. A rodentologist is a type of biologist. They study rodents like mice and rats. Can anyone think of any other types of biologists?"

Frankie put her hand up. She knew all kinds of biologists. Ms. Cupid called on Luke, who said, "A bugologist?"

"Great!" Ms. Cupid said. Frankie was pretty sure that "great" was Ms. Cupid's favorite word. She used it all the time. "A biologist who studies insects is called an entomologist." She wrote that word down on the chart paper in her neat, straight print. "Anyone else?"

"Maybe a herpetologist?" Ravi asked. He didn't even stumble over the big word.

"Yes!" Ms. Cupid cheered. "And what's a herpetologist?"

"Someone who studies lizards and amphibians."

Suki asked, "How about someone who studies fish?"

"Oh! Terrific, Suki! This is actually one of my all-time top-ten favorite words. *Ichthyologist*. Can everyone say that?"

The class stumbled over the word as they tried to say it back to her. "We'll work on it. We have plenty of time." She put down her pointer and looked right at Frankie. "I'm so glad you shared this today, because it's just perfect for something we are going to do later. I was going to tell you after snack, but I think I'll spill my secret now." She smiled, and the silver in her braces sparkled. Frankie hadn't even known that grown-ups could have braces, but Ms. Cupid did, and Frankie thought they were as beautiful on her teeth as any jewelry. "We are all going to be biologists. We are going to study animals. And after we study animals, we are going to have a very important decision to make." She stood up and walked over to a big rectangle covered by bright fabric with paw prints all over it. She pulled the fabric off and revealed a large glass aquarium, just like the ones the lizards had lived in at Aunt Gina's lab. "Friends," she announced, "we are going to research different kinds of animals, because we are going to get a class pet."

CHAPTER 2

All about Rodents

THE CLASS ERUPTED. MAYA GRABBED on to Frankie's arm and cried, "No way!"

Lila said, "We have to get a girl pet so that we have equal boys and girls."

"A dog? Can we get a dog?"

"A dog can't live in an aquarium. It has to be a fish."

"Or a hermit crab."

Frankie was an island of calm in all this

madness. She sat, as still as a toadstool, with a big smile on her face. She knew exactly what should go in that case. A rodent. They were going to get a pet rodent.

Ms. Cupid held up her hand so that her thumb pressed her middle two fingers against her palm and her pointer and pinky stood up like ears. "Quiet coyote is asking for calm."

The class settled their voices.

"It is very exciting news," Ms. Cupid agreed. "But we have a lot to do before it can happen. We need to research different kinds of pets and prepare arguments. We'll have to convince Principal Flower that we can take care of a pet. We have to figure out how much things like food and supplies will cost."

Frankie nodded as Ms. Cupid spoke, but

she was busy thinking of all the different rodents she had seen with Aunt Gina. Since they couldn't get anything as big as a capybara, Frankie thought she might like a rat. Aunt Gina had told her they were very smart. Even a simple mouse would be great, but she bet Maya would like a guinea pig. It had big eyes and a cute face. Maya loved cats, and since of course they couldn't get a pet cat for school, a guinea pig would be the next best thing since it was kind of roly-poly like a kitten.

"For now, though," Ms. Cupid continued, "we need to finish up morning meeting, and then we will have our reading block."

Frankie kept her eyes on Ms. Cupid, but she had a hard time listening, and she almost missed the direction to go back to her table.

She grabbed Maya's hand. "Let's choose Read Together, okay?"

Maya stopped at her own table and glanced at the thick novel that sat at her place. "I was thinking about choosing Read to Self, but sure, okay. What do you want to read?"

Waiting at Frankie's seat was a book her aunt had given her: *All about Rodents.*

"Oh," Maya said. "That looks interesting." Maya had dark hair that went halfway down her back. She twirled the ends around her fingers. "Want to sit in the beanbags?"

Frankie agreed, and the two friends huddled together on one beanbag. "Isn't this so exciting?" Frankie asked. "A class pet!"

Maya brightened. "I know! I've never had a class pet before. My mom told me her nursery school had a guinea pig and it bit her!"

"Girls, let's get reading," Ms. Cupid reminded them.

So Frankie opened the book. "'Rodents,'" she read out loud, "'are mammals. They are chara—charac—'" The word stopped her.

"'Characterized,'" Maya finished for her. Then she said it again, more slowly. "'Char-ac-ter-ized.'"

"'They are characterized by incis—'"

"'Incisors,'" Maya finished for her.

"Right." Frankie pointed to her own two front teeth. "These are your incisors. They are your cutting teeth." Frankie knew what a lot of words meant, but sometimes she had trouble reading them when they were down on paper. She started reading again. "'Rodents are mammals. They are characterized by incisors that never stop growing. Rodents are the largest group of mammals.'"

"Wait? Their teeth just keep getting bigger and bigger?" Maya asked.

"Yeah!" Frankie answered excitedly. "That's why they always need something to chew on.

Otherwise their teeth can get too big for their mouths!" She held up two fingers in front of her mouth like they were long rat's teeth.

Maya wrinkled her nose and turned the page of the book. "'There are many different kinds of rodents,'" she read. Frankie loved to do Read Together with Maya, and not just because they were best friends. When Maya read, it was like the words danced out of her. It was almost like listening to a teacher read. "'Some rodents, like mice, are very small. Others can be very large. The marmot, for example, can grow up to two feet long, not including its tail!'"

"Huh," Frankie said. "Do you think something that big would fit in that aquarium?"

Maya glanced up at the aquarium that still

sat on the table at the front of the room. "That can't be bigger than three feet across. I think that wouldn't be very nice for the marmot."

"You're probably right. I guess we'll have to get a smaller rodent."

"For a class pet, you mean?"

"Yeah. It's okay. There are lots and lots of smaller rodents. Mice, hamsters, gerbils—all sorts of things. I'm sure we can find one that will fit."

Maya twirled her hair again. It was what Frankie's mom called a nervous habit, but Frankie had no clue what Maya might be nervous about. "What if we don't get a rodent?" Maya asked.

"Of course we're going to get a rodent! All the rodents at my aunt's university live in aquariums just like that. Well, I mean, the bigger ones live in bigger cages, but like I said, we can get a smaller rodent."

Maya chewed on her lip. "I guess I just hadn't considered a rodent."

Frankie wrapped her arm around Maya's shoulders. "It's good that we're such great friends, then. I thought of it for both of us!"

"Right," Maya said, and gave Frankie a small smile.

"Go on," Frankie urged. "Read me more about the marmot. I want to hear about it even though we can't get one."

So Maya kept reading about how marmots build burrows under boulder fields and rocky cliffs. Then they read about how some rodents had pouches in their cheeks to carry food back to their homes. They learned that rodents had been around for almost fifty-six million years. Together they read most of the book before the reading block was over. When they were finished, Frankie was more certain than ever that a rodent was the perfect pet for Ms. Cupid's third-grade classroom.

CHAPTER 3

Parameters
of the Problem

THE CLASS PET WAS ALL ANYONE could talk about during snack, and during lunch and recess. Normally while Frankie waited for her turn in four-square, she tapped her feet impatiently. But on the day of the class-pet announcement, she made lists of rodents in her mind. By the time they came back inside, red-faced and sweaty, Frankie had settled it.

Her first choice would be a rat. They were very smart animals, so you could teach them tricks. Sometimes they would even come when you called their names.

She put her coat back into her cubby. Ravi had the cubby next to hers. "What kind of animal do you want?" he asked.

"Rat," she answered.

He nodded. "Good choice. Personally, I'm thinking of a mouse. I'm going to teach it to ride a toy motorcycle like in that book Ms. Adams read to us last year. *The Mouse and the Motorcycle.*"

"That was fiction, Ravi," she told him. "You can't teach a mouse to ride a motorcycle." But all the while she wondered if maybe she could teach a rat to ride something, like

maybe a little toy car that he powered with his feet.

Ravi just shrugged and went to the carpet, where the rest of the class had already settled. Frankie had to take a seat on the corner of the carpet, far away from Maya.

Ms. Cupid was sitting in her rocking chair next to the easel with a big piece of chart paper. "We are going to brainstorm about class pets," Ms. Cupid explained. "We are going to try to come up with a list of possible animals."

Frankie shot her hand up into the air. Ms. Cupid held up one finger, which Frankie knew meant that she had to wait.

"Before we can brainstorm, we need to think about what kind of animal we might be allowed to get," Ms. Cupid went on. "We need to come up with some guidelines to help us narrow our focus. Sometimes we call these 'parameters.'"

Frankie knew what Ms. Cupid was talking about. Her mom worked for a technology company that made robots and computers to solve problems. She always said that the first step was to define "the parameters of the problem."

Ms. Cupid wrote the word "parameters" at the top of the sheet of chart paper. "First, the pet we get needs to be able to fit in this aquarium."

That made sense, Frankie thought as she watched Ms. Cupid write the first parameter on the chart paper.

"Number two, the price of the animal itself must be less than fifty dollars." Ms. Cupid wrote as she spoke, which Frankie thought was a very impressive thing to be able to do.

Frankie knew that the cost of a rat wouldn't be a problem. Rats and other small rodents weren't very expensive at all. The class would need to get other things for the cage, though. She raised her hand. "Just the animal, or anything else we need?" she asked when Ms. Cupid called on her.

"Good question. We have fifty dollars to spend total. Food, of course, will be an ongoing expense, but anything we need to get the pet set up has to be included in that fifty dollars."

Ravi raised his hand. "What's going to happen to the animal when we're on vacation?"

Ms. Cupid tapped her nose. "Good question. Thoughts, everyone?"

"We bring our dog to the kennel," Suki told the class. "Maybe we can bring our class pet to a kennel over vacation."

"We'd need money for that," Luke argued. "How about we take turns bringing it home?"

Frankie about fell over at that. A rat? At her house? That would be amazing! "We can definitely take it at my house!" she exclaimed.

Ms. Cupid nodded. "Good thinking. I am going to say that I can take the class pet home over vacations, or maybe it will get to visit some of your homes. In that case, the pet needs to be easily portable. We also can't be bringing it back and forth each week. So our pet will need to be one that can be left alone for the weekend."

"We leave my cat home alone some week-ends," Luke said.

"We can't put a cat in an aquarium," Ravi replied.

"True." Ms. Cupid agreed. "But I think Luke is getting at a good point. He can leave his cat at home because the cat can take care of itself. It can go get itself some food, and it has a place to go to the bathroom, and it has plenty of space to move around in the house. A dog, on the other hand, is not good to leave at home, right?"

"Right," Suki agreed. "We need to feed our dog every day."

"And you don't want it to poop in the house!" Luke exclaimed.

Frankie was only half listening to this conversation. She was imagining all the tricks she would teach the rat.

"So," Ms. Cupid said, "I think we can add some details to our last parameter. It should be an animal that doesn't need to be fed every day."

She added this to her list, which now read:

PARAMETERS

1. Fits in aquarium.

2. Costs less than $50.

3. Easily portable.

4. Able to be alone for the weekend—does not need to be fed every day.

Frankie looked over the list. *Fits in the aquarium?* Check. That aquarium would be a palace for a rat. *Costs less than fifty dollars?* Check. She was pretty sure that rats cost much less than fifty dollars. *Easily portable?* Check. It could travel in its aquarium—or in her pocket. *Able to be alone for the weekend—does not need to be fed every day?* She bit her lip. She wasn't sure about this one. Her aunt had told her that there were college students who worked in the lab every day. Some even came in on weekends to make sure the animals were okay. But did the rodents *need* to eat every day? She was pretty sure they did.

She felt her stomach sinking. So she pressed right on her belly. *Frankie Sparks, you are a problem solver,* she told herself. She needed to get a little more information, and of course she knew just who to ask. As soon as she got home, she would call Aunt Gina, and she'd get the facts. If a rat did need to be fed every day, well then, Frankie would figure out a solution for that.

"So right now I want everyone to think of three different animals that could meet these parameters. You might not know yet if it costs less than fifty dollars or if it can go a whole weekend alone. We will do some research tomorrow. For now, write down ideas of animals that you think could work. Three animals, three sticky notes. Got it?"

Frankie picked up her pencil. She wrote as neatly as she could. Sometimes, as careful as she was, her letters still came out wobbly. But this time they were pretty clear. *Rat,* she wrote on one sticky note. *Hampster,* she wrote on another. That didn't look right. She crossed it out and wrote *hamster.* She tapped her pencil against her lips. "Guinea pig" was even harder to spell, but she did her best: *Ginnee Pig.* She figured Ms. Cupid

would know what she meant. Ms. Cupid was pretty good about that sort of thing.

When they were finished, Ms. Cupid told them to find a buddy and try to sort their animals into types. Then the partners would combine with another pair for a group of four, and then again for a group of eight, until they had all the animal ideas sorted. Frankie went straight to Maya. Maya's Post-its were all lined up. Her handwriting never wobbled.

Betta fish. Hermit crab. Goldfish.

Frankie could not believe her eyes!

"What about a rat?" Frankie asked.

Maya looked at Frankie's pile. She looked back up at Frankie without a smile. She wasn't frowning, either. In fact Frankie would have said her expression was worse than a frown.

Her lips were all wiggly, and she wouldn't look Frankie in the eye. Was it possible that Maya didn't want a rat?

"How about a gerbil?" Frankie asked. "They're really cute!"

Maya didn't answer. Was it possible she didn't want a rodent at all?

"A hamster?"

"I guess they could be kind of adorable," Maya agreed.

Frankie grinned from ear to ear. Maya was Frankie's best friend, and Frankie knew one thing for certain: Maya would be on her side when it came to making sure the class pet was a rodent. Now she just had to convince the rest of the class.

CHAPTER 4

The Expert

FRANKIE'S MOM MET HER AT THE bottom of the school's front steps. They walked down the street together toward their house. The sun shone as brightly as a lemon hanging in the sky. "Mom!" Frankie exclaimed. "You will never believe the most wonderful thing that happened today."

"A UFO landed in the playground?"

"No."

"It was make-your-own-sundae day for lunch?"

Frankie smiled, but she was also bubbling over, ready to tell her mother about the class pet and how they were going to get a rodent. "No. It was—"

"Wait! I've got it! You got to do coding during your library time!"

"No!" Frankie exclaimed, ready to burst. "We're going to get a pet rodent for our class!"

"Really? Your aunt Gina will be excited to hear that. Maybe she could come into school to help you learn about it."

"Do you think she would do that?"

"Sure! She owes me about a million favors. Plus, you are her favorite niece."

"I'm her *only* niece."

Frankie's mom opened their front door, and they went inside the warm house. "She loves you, and she loves talking about rodents. You probably won't be able to get her out of the school."

Frankie dropped her backpack onto the ground and went straight to the refrigerator to get an apple for a snack. "Can I call her to get some information? We're supposed to find out what you need to take care of a rodent."

"Is that your homework?"

Frankie shook her head. "No. I have a math worksheet."

"Do that first, and then you can call. She might be teaching, though."

Frankie tried to eat her apple like a rat. She held it in both hands and nibbled away at it

with quick bites. It was taking a long time.
While she nibbled, she worked on her math
sheet. When she finished, her mom passed
her the phone. Her mom had already dialed
and the phone was ringing. "Dr. Parker speaking," her aunt answered the phone.

"We're getting a rodent in
our classroom!" Frankie
explained. "I need you
to tell me everything
we need to know about
having a rodent."

"Frankie?" her aunt
asked.

"Yes, of course."

"How about a hello?"

"Hello, Aunt Gina."

"How are you, Frankie?"

"I'm fine. How are you?" Frankie didn't understand why grown-ups always wanted to say "Hello" and "How are you?" and not get right down to business.

"I'm well, Frankie. Now, what can I help you with?"

"We're getting a rodent, and I want to get a rat because they're so smart. But our rule is that it has to be something that doesn't need to be fed every day. Do you feed your rats every day?"

"Slow down, Frankie. One thing at a time. You need to make an argument about what type of rodent to get?"

"Yes, that's right."

"And you want a rat?"

Frankie sighed. She loved her aunt, but Aunt Gina was one of those people who liked to take things slowly. She was not grasping the urgency of the situation. "Yes, Aunt Gina. I want a rat. I want to teach it tricks."

"You said there were rules. What are they? What are the limits here?"

Frankie answered quickly. "It has to fit in

an aquarium. A smallish aquarium. Maybe three feet."

"That leaves out a lot," Aunt Gina said. Frankie could just picture her walking around her lab full of rodents. How lucky she was to spend all day with them!

"Like marmots," said Frankie. "Those would be way too big."

"Precisely." Aunt Gina laughed. "What are the other guidelines?"

"Less than fifty dollars."

"Okay, we're good there. Plenty of inexpensive rodents. What else?"

"Easily transportable. We need to be able to take it home over vacations and such."

"Got it," she said. "Anything else?"

"Just the not-needing-to-be-fed-every-day thing. It needs to be more like a cat and less like a dog."

"I can't say I'm an expert in either feline or canine behavior, but I think I see where you're going here."

"I really want a rat, Aunt Gina. So I need to know if they get fed every day."

There was silence on the other end of the line.

"Aunt Gina?" Frankie asked. "Are you still there?"

"Your teacher told you to find out about a rodent that could be a class pet and go the weekend without food?" she asked Frankie.

Frankie bit her lip. She traced her toe along the floor. "She didn't say it had to be a rodent, precisely. People are researching all different kinds of animals. Maya wants a fish. Isn't that crazy?"

"Fish don't need to be fed every day," Aunt Gina told her.

Frankie looked down at her notebook. She had been drawing pictures of gerbils and rats. Now her stomach started to turn and twist like a tangle of shoelaces.

"Frankie, there just aren't many rodents that make good classroom pets in the first place, and all of those definitely eat every day."

"Couldn't we just leave an extra-big pile of food?"

"You could. But it's better that they get fresh pellets every day. They can be pretty picky. They'll eat the old pellets, but they won't be happy about it. And you want a happy rodent, right?"

Frankie sat down in her chair. "Yes," she sighed.

"Frankie, you are sounding deflated."

"I *am* deflated, Aunt Gina!"

"That doesn't sound like the Frankie Sparks I know and love. Where's your can-do spirit? Where's your problem-solving drive?"

Frankie sat up a little bit. Her aunt was right. Wasn't that what she had told herself earlier? There wasn't a problem she couldn't solve. "You're right, Aunt Gina."

"I know," she replied. "I typically am." Frankie could picture Aunt Gina's big smile. She had the kind of smile that showed all her shiny teeth. "Let me give you one thing to noodle on, Frankie. A rat needs to *eat* every day, and it should be *fed* every day, but it doesn't need to be fed by you."

"Is that a riddle?" Frankie asked.

"It's a challenge."

Frankie grinned. There were few things she loved more than a challenge, and she knew that the first step to meeting a challenge was finding out as much information as she could.

CHAPTER 5

Disappointments

THE SHEETS OF CHART PAPER THAT Ms. Cupid put around the room were big and yellow, the color of lemon sherbet. They were so sunny and friendly-looking that Frankie could almost forget that she still hadn't figured out how to feed the rat on the weekends. "Yesterday we started a list of animals that we could have for a class pet."

Rat, Frankie thought. *Rat, rat, rat.* She

would write the word on every single piece of yellow chart paper. She would write it neatly and she would spell it correctly, and on each sheet she would use a different-colored pen so that people would think that different kids had come up with the same idea. Her fingers itched, ready to spread the word throughout the classroom.

"Today we are going to start research," Ms. Cupid announced. "We are going to focus on figuring out which animals meet our parameters. Ms. Appleton is going to come down with some library books about animals and some great websites she found. We will start a list of possible animals to have as pets. Animals that meet all four criteria we set out."

Frankie sat on her hands and rocked back

and forth. She had done her research already! She wanted to announce this to the class, but that would be blurting, and Ms. Cupid hated blurting. Plus, Frankie still hadn't figured out how to feed the rat fresh food over the weekend. Aunt Gina's challenge stuck in her mind: *A rat needs to* eat *every day, and it should be* fed *every day, but it doesn't need to be fed by you.* Janitors worked at the school. Maybe they could feed it?

Ms. Cupid locked eyes with Frankie. It was like she had special radar for when Frankie's mind was wandering. Frankie wished she could send a message back to her, but it didn't seem to work.

Luckily, Ms. Appleton knocked on the classroom window just then. Frankie leaped to her feet and opened the door. Ms. Apple-ton pushed in one of her library carts and exclaimed, "Hello, friends!" She gave a quick explanation of the books she'd brought and told the class to visit the library website for links to good web pages about animals. She handed out a graphic organizer worksheet and explained how they were supposed to use it to take notes.

When it was finally time to start research-ing, the rest of the class picked up books or laptops, but Frankie went straight to her cubby. She had been busy the night before!

"Ms. Cupid!" Frankie called as she hurried to the front of the room. "Look what I did!" She thrust a stack of papers toward her teacher.

"What's that, Frankie?"

"Research about rats. I did all my research, and I'm ready to make my argument. Do I get extra points for being so quick? Can I share my argument with the class today? Maybe we could go ahead and just decide today."

"Oh, Frankie, we aren't ready to decide yet."

"But once people hear about rats, they won't want to get anything else."

"I'm sorry, Frankie, but that's not the way this is going to work. We're going to spend a lot of time on this. Today is a research day."

"But I already did my research. My aunt gave me a book when I saw her last weekend, and I read all the words about the rats, and I wrote down all the facts."

"That's great, Frankie. I think Ms. Appleton is going to show us some websites to look at too."

"But I read all the words, Ms. Cupid. All by myself."

Ms. Cupid put down Frankie's notes. "I really am proud of you, Frankie. And I am glad that you are so excited about this project. But we need to give everyone a chance to get just as excited as you are."

"Ms. Cupid, this is a huge disappointment."

"I'm sorry you feel that way." She actually did look sorry about it, but that didn't make Frankie feel any better. In fact it made her feel worse, because it meant that nothing was going to change. Ms. Cupid felt bad, but not bad enough to let Frankie go ahead and make her argument. Ms. Cupid was going to stick to her plan no matter what.

With her head hung low, Frankie went and slumped into the chair next to Maya, even though Ms. Cupid had put them at different tables this week. She sighed heavily. Maya looked up from her graphic organizer. Frankie noticed that Maya had already answered nearly all the questions. Frankie sighed again.

"What's wrong?" Maya asked.

"I spent all night taking notes about rats. Did you know they can survive being flushed down a toilet?"

"I didn't know that," Maya said. "That's a little bit cool and a little bit gross."

"Exactly!" Frankie exclaimed.

"So why are you upset?"

"Well, I took all these notes and I'm ready to make my argument, but Ms. Cupid says I have to wait. I have to wait for everyone else to do research and make their own arguments. It's not fair."

"It's kind of fair," Maya murmured. "I'd like a chance to make an argument about an animal too."

Frankie stared at her friend with her eyes wide. She could not believe what she was hearing. "But you know what animal you want. You want a rat."

"No, Frankie. *You* want a rat. I think we should get a fish, something pretty. I just don't know which one yet. I like bettas, but—"

"A fish?" Frankie asked. Here was what Frankie knew about fish: They died. Not always, and not immediately, but in terms of life span, a fish's was pretty short.

Also, fish were boring.

Ms. Appleton, the school librarian, might have said this was an opinion, not a fact, but Frankie would disagree. Fish were *factually* boring.

"I like fish," Maya said. "I think they're interesting." As she spoke, she drew a small fish on the bottom of her worksheet.

"But all they do is swim—back and forth, back and forth."

Betta fish   Betta splendens

"I like watching them swim. I am on the swim team, you know. And anyway, I like the way their fins move in the water. I think it's kind of beautiful. I saw a yellow one in the store. It made me think of a flower. If we got a yellow betta fish, I'd name it Buttercup."

Frankie just stared at Maya. Maya stared back. Frankie felt like an old, flat bouncing ball that had been left in the sun on the playground. She and Maya almost never disagreed.

Frankie got up and went back to her table. Ms. Cupid had left a math worksheet for her with a note: *Here's some fun math for you to do while everyone else catches up!* Ms. Cupid had drawn a heart on the note. Normally Frankie loved math, but this was a time-telling worksheet. She hated practicing telling time because she hated clocks. Fat hands and skinny hands spinning by the numbers. They always went slowly when you wanted them to go quickly and quickly when you wanted them to go slowly.

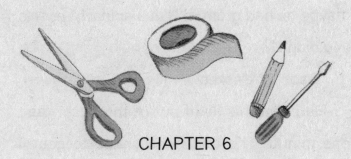

CHAPTER 6

The Unfairness of It All

FRANKIE'S FATHER HAD HIS HEAD deep into a leafy bush, which made it hard for Frankie to have a serious conversation with him. All she could see were his back and shoulders and the bottoms of his work boots, which were caked in mud. "Can't you please come out of there?" she asked him.

Frankie's dad just grunted. It sounded like

maybe he had grunted "I'm a spinach" or "No you didn't."

"Dad?" she asked.

He pulled his head out of the bush. "Just one minute," he told her. "I need to get all these shoots at the base tugged together so that this beauty grows up instead of out." With that he disappeared into the bush again. Her father ran a nursery—the kind for plants, not for kids. On the days when her mom had to go into the office in the city for a meeting or a presentation, Frankie rode the bus to Sparks Nursery after school and helped her father. She liked some of the jobs, like watering plants or picking the old dead buds off the rhododendrons. But other parts were less fun, like how her dad never had any good snacks. Only beef jerky, which Frankie thought tasted like the tongue of an old man's shoe.

Finally her father emerged from the plant. "I thought you were excited about getting a class pet."

"I am," Frankie sighed. "Which is why I did all that work, and Ms. Cupid didn't even care, and Maya wants a fish."

"Oh, I like fish. What kind of fish does she want? Did you know that there are fish that work in aquaponics? You grow a little plant on top of the fish tank. It provides some food for the fish and helps to keep the tank clean. Win-win."

"Dad!" Frankie interrupted. "I don't want a fish. I want a rat."

"That does seem to be a problem." He put his hands on his knees.

"Well, it wouldn't be a problem if Ms. Cupid would just act the way a teacher is supposed to act. I read through almost all of the book that Aunt Gina gave me, and I looked up the hard words and everything, and Ms. Cupid didn't even look at my notes. And she definitely didn't let me make my argument to the class. I have a very good argument."

"I'm sure you do. I bet that's very upsetting." He scratched his beard.

"No one else really cares, not enough to even find out the most basic details about the animals. Maya doesn't even know what kind of fish she wants."

Her father held up both his hands, which

were brown with dirt. "Wait. Are we mad at Ms. Cupid or at Maya?"

"I'm mad about the unfairness of it all!" Frankie declared, throwing up her own hands.

"I see," he said. He had deep brown eyes that Frankie thought looked like chocolate pudding, and when he looked right at her, it usually made her feel better. This time even chocolate-pudding eyes didn't seem to help. "When I'm feeling frustrated, I dig into my work."

Frankie tried not to smile at his pun. She was feeling good and angry, and sometimes when she was feeling good and angry, she didn't want to let that feeling go.

"You've been thinking about this problem for a while now, Frankie," her dad said. "Maybe you should think about something else."

"Like what?" she demanded.

Frankie's dad frowned, and Frankie knew that there was going to be a talking-to. "It seems like you're in a mood. Go for a walk," he suggested. "Go for a run. Go move the terra-cotta pots around. Get it all out of you, and then maybe we can talk."

Frankie knew in a deep, deep part of her that her dad was probably right. She was mad and she should go do something else. Instead she stood up from the bucket she'd been perched on and walked off in a huff. There was a certain satisfaction in walking off in a huff, and she was pretty good at it. She gave a loud sigh and stomped her feet so that they made *thud, thud, thud* sounds as she marched away. But then she was all alone. She was still angry, but she had no one to be angry with or angry at. She marched back and forth down the aisles of the nursery, staring at her feet and her scuffed sneakers instead of at the plants or where she was going, which was how she almost marched right into Ravi and his mother.

Ravi's mother wore one of her beautiful

saris, which was made of silk and woven through with gold thread. Frankie jammed her hands into her pockets to keep from touching it.

"Hi, Frankie!" Ravi greeted her. He smiled, but Frankie was in such a sour mood that the smile seemed like he was making fun of her anger.

"Hey," she replied.

"Hello, Frankie," Mrs. Reddy said. "You look like you are stewing over something. Is everything all right?"

Frankie kicked the dirt, which only scuffed her shoes even more. "I'm fine," she answered.

"She's mad because she wants a rat for the class pet and Maya wants a fish and Ms. Cupid isn't even ready to start deciding," Ravi declared.

"How'd you know all that?" Frankie asked him.

"I pay attention," he told her. He looked back at his mom. "She's also mad because she and Maya are having a fight because Frankie's trying to convince Maya to vote for a rat and Maya wants a fish."

Frankie scowled.

"Anyway, I wanted a bearded dragon—"

"I thought you wanted a mouse," Frankie said.

"I *did*," he replied. "But you're right. It probably can't ride a motorcycle. And anyway, then I read about bearded dragons, and they seem pretty amazing. But they're too big. So then I was thinking of leopard geckos. They shed their skin and eat it."

"Whoa!" Frankie didn't mean to be impressed, but she was.

Leopard gecko
Eublepharis macularius

"So geckos are my first choice, but I think a rat could be cool too."

"I did all this reading about rats last night, about how to take care of them, and what they eat, and what we would need if we had a rat. I wrote it all down in my neatest handwriting. I even had my main idea and three supporting pieces of evidence, just like we learned, but

Ms. Cupid wouldn't even listen to me for one second. Not one millisecond."

"I think she listened for at least ten seconds," Ravi said. "Maybe even thirty."

Frankie scowled.

"That must have been very disappointing," Mrs. Reddy told her. "Would you like to present your argument to me?"

"Right now?"

"Sure, why not? It will give you practice for when Ms. Cupid is ready for you to make your case."

This made a lot of sense to Frankie. Frankie took a deep breath and then began her speech. "Do you know how smart rats are? They can learn to follow mazes, they can press a button to get a treat, and they can even learn to sit and shake hands, like a dog. They like to play and are active. They keep themselves clean, just like a cat, and if we get more than one rat, they will clean each other. So we won't have to worry about giving them baths. We would have to clean the cage, but that's pretty easy. You just empty out the old bedding, wipe down the cage, and then put new bedding in. It could be someone's classroom job. Rats are very social and friendly and make a cute noise when they are happy."

When she finished, Ravi nodded. "Okay, I think you have me convinced to be on Team Rat."

"Really?" she asked.

"Sure. But there's one big problem, Frankie: If it has to be fed every day, Ms. Cupid won't even consider it. You know the guidelines. I guess it's back to the gecko for me. Do you think we could get a piranha? She never said no carnivores."

"I'm pretty sure piranhas aren't allowed in school."

"You're probably right. Maybe I'll just go along with Luke and the hermit crab. Unless, of course, you know of some rodent that can feed itself." Ravi laughed at his joke, and his mom tsk-tsked him.

Frankie, though, leaped toward him, clapping her hands. "Ravi!" she cried. "You are a genius!"

Ravi hadn't realized it, but he had given Frankie the best idea ever. Now she knew exactly what she had to do.

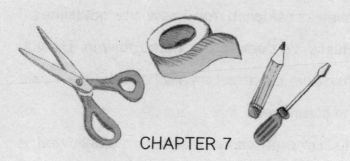

CHAPTER 7

Designing a Solution

IT WAS TIME TO HEAD TO HER INVENT-
ing lab. The lab had been a closet, but she
and her parents had cleaned everything out
of it. She had a small worktable with a stool
that rolled beneath it. Above the table hung a
pegboard full of tools, and below were stack-
ing crates full of cardboard scraps, LEGO
bricks, wires, and more. Most of her supplies

had been rescued from the family recycling bin. Her lab was where she made all her inventions. And she had a lot of them.

There was the Horn Helper, a special device to go onto a unicorn's horn so that it could pick up trash at the beach. That had been a great invention, aside from not being able to find a unicorn to test it. Another favorite was her Perfect Pancakers. Frankie loved to help her dad make breakfast on the weekends, and she had invented a special scoop that picked up just the right number of blueberries or chocolate chips and then dropped them onto the pancakes. It worked better than stirring them into the batter, plus she got to make construction-truck sounds while she used it, since it looked and worked a lot like an excavator. She still had the prototype for that one, made out of an old toy truck, sitting on her shelf. And then there was the Color-Changing Cap. She had made that for Maya. It was a swim cap with lights on it that blinked all different colors. She'd sewn the lights on. Maya couldn't wear it in the pool, of course, but she had looked the coolest in the team pictures.

Frankie bit her lip when she thought about Maya. It didn't feel good to have her best friend mad at her. It felt like opening up a box of cereal and finding only dust and broken flakes. It felt like playing with a paper airplane that always dropped straight to the ground. But Frankie had only been trying to help! She knew that

Maya would be disappointed when the boring betta fish didn't get picked. She was trying to get Maya onto the winning team.

The twinge in her stomach told her maybe that wasn't 100 percent true.

She took a deep breath. What she needed to do was figure out how to feed this rat. Then maybe Maya would understand. Maybe Maya would even decide to vote for the rat all on her own.

Ravi's words still rang in her brain: *Unless you know of some rodent that can feed itself.* That was the solution! It was just like Aunt Gina had said: The rat needed to be fed every day, but she didn't need to feed it. The rat could feed itself! She went back to her pile of notes. *Rats are very smart,* she read in her own wobbly handwriting. *They are used in experiments. They are trained to do things like come when called, fetch, and press a button for food.*

Frankie grinned. She had her solution. She needed to make it so the rat could feed itself by pushing a button! Luckily, she was the world's best third-grade inventor, so she knew that with a little work she'd be able to design a rat self-feeder. In the pictures she had seen online and in books, the button seemed to open up a hatch that let the food drop down. That would take levers and springs. She thought she might need to do something a little simpler.

She took out a blank piece of paper and

Brown rat or Norway rat
Rattus norvegicus

drew a small rat and its food bowl. "How can I get the food to drop down into there?" She drew a little bucket and wrote the word "food" on it. If the rat could tip the bucket some-how, then it could feed itself. *Easy enough,* she thought. She drew little arrows to show how the bucket would move and how it would dump the food.

Next it was time to make a prototype,

which was another word that Frankie liked a lot. A prototype was like the rough draft of a paper—the kind you turn into a teacher for feedback before you make it better. With her prototype she'd be able to test her design and make sure it worked.

She dug through her crate and pulled out the cardboard tube from an empty roll of toilet paper. She always kept them for her building. She hummed and tapped her lips as she looked at the various options in the recycling crate. What could work as the bucket? A shoebox? No, too big. A plastic container from the deli? That might work to stand in for the rat's food dish. When she picked it up, she saw a snack-size yogurt container underneath. Perfect! She gave it a sniff—100 percent clean!

Her wire spool hung on the pegboard right next to the wire cutters. Her mom had taught her how to use the wire cutters, and she carefully trimmed off two pieces, each about six inches long. It was hard to poke holes in the yogurt container, but she managed. She twined the wire through each part until the yogurt container hung off of the toilet paper tube like the basket of a hot-air balloon. She pushed up the bottom of the yogurt cup and it tilted down. Simple but effective—those were the best kind of inventions, she thought. The tube would send the food down into the bucket, then the rat would tip the bucket when it was hungry.

Frankie's family didn't have any pets, so she didn't have any pet food she could use.

Maya had a friendly old dog named Opus and a shy cat named Delilah. If she and Maya hadn't been fighting, she could have gone over to get some pet food from their house. Frankie frowned. But she let herself be down for only a minute. She decided to use rice instead of pellets when she tested her design. As soon as she started dumping in the rice, she realized a problem: The tube was supposed to help get the food into the cup, but instead the rice spilled out of the tube and onto her table. Some went into the yogurt cup, but a lot went out. She tightened up the wire so that the cup was closer to the tube. Now when she tried, the rice went in easily, and when she tilted the cup, the rice poured out perfectly.

Frankie clapped her hands and ran out of her lab. She almost smacked right into her dad. "Whoa there. Where's the fire?"

"Testing phase!" Frankie announced.

"What are you making?" he asked. "Is it for the rat?"

"Sure is!" she replied.

Her dad grinned. "That's my Frankie! I told you that you just needed to get busy."

Frankie started running again. Her socks slid on the floor as she rounded the corner to the hall and sprinted to her bedroom.

Her stuffed animals were all in a big basket. She tossed them out one after another. Bear, dog, penguin. "Where *is* it?" she exclaimed. Elephant, another dog, hippo.

Finally, at the very bottom, she found what she was looking for: a small mouse dressed in a suit coat with shiny black buttons. One year Maya's family had taken Maya and Frankie to see the *Nutcracker* and had bought them toys. Maya had gotten a Clara doll, and Frankie had chosen this soldier. Why did everything remind her of Maya and the fight they were having?

Mouse in hand, she ran back to her lab.

Standing at her desk, she took a deep breath. "Hi," she said, speaking for the mouse. "I may look like a mouse in a fancy jacket, but really I'm a rat, and I am very hungry." She hopped the mouse along the table. In her other hand she held up her invention. "What's this? Hmm, smells like food." She lifted the stuffed mouse so that it could tip the yogurt cup. The invention worked! And the cup dumped the rice all over the mouse.

"Whoops!" Frankie exclaimed.

She figured a rat, no matter how hungry it was, wouldn't want to have the food dumped all over him. After all, there were days when all she could think about was pizza, but she didn't want to show up at Farmington House of Pizza and have a pepperoni pie thrown in her face.

The solution came to her pretty quickly. She took a Popsicle stick and duct tape—two of an inventor's greatest tools—and taped the stick flat to the bottom of the yogurt container. Now the rat could come up from behind the container, push up on the stick like a lever, and dump out the food, safe from harm. She grinned. She added a cap to the top of the tube to keep the food extra fresh, and *bam!* Her prototype was complete.

CHAPTER 8

Fish Facts

FRANKIE KEPT HER LIPS SEALED AT school. She wasn't going to tell anyone about her invention until the day of the presentations. So the next morning, when Ms. Cupid handed out a new graphic organizer, Frankie dutifully filled it out. The worksheet was divided into five sections: size, costs, habitat, food, and fun facts. Frankie brought it back up to Ms. Cupid, who smiled and said, "Frankie has finished, so she can be a helper. If you need help, raise your hand."

Frankie beamed. She usually took a long time to finish classwork, so she didn't get to be a helper very often. Only when they used computers to make things, because she was fast with those. But never for reading and writing. She wished that Ms. Cupid had a badge that she could wear. It would be shaped like a star and would say GRAPHIC ORGANIZER on it in glittery letters—probably purple ones, since Ms. Cupid loved purple.

"Frankie," Ms. Cupid whispered, popping her dream bubble. "I think Maya could use some help."

"Maya?" Frankie asked with a frown.

"Yes," Ms. Cupid answered.

Clearly, Ms. Cupid didn't know that Maya

and Frankie were having a fight. But you couldn't just say no to a teacher, so Frankie walked across the room. She walked very slowly, touching each tile along the way and checking in with everyone she passed. Finally she had no choice but to sit down at the table next to Maya. "Ms. Cupid says I need to help you."

Maya looked up sharply, first at Frankie and then at Ms. Cupid. "I'm fine," Maya replied. "I don't need any help."

Maya's graphic organizer, though, was empty. "You look like you could use some help," Frankie told her.

Across the room Ravi wrote furiously on his paper. Frankie wondered what animal he was writing about. Had he really gone back to Team Gecko? Didn't he want a rat too? Maybe the whole class was going to turn against her!

"This website says the betta fish lives two to three years," Maya told her, pointing at the computer screen. "But I don't know where to write that on here."

"In three years we'll be in middle school," Frankie replied.

"So?" Maya asked. "I still think it's important for Ms. Cupid to know."

Frankie thought about this. She supposed it was important for Ms. Cupid to know what she was getting into. Rats lived for two to three years, but the world-record rat had lived for more than seven years. "Short is good. Ms. Cupid is a young teacher now, but in twenty years she'll be ancient," Frankie explained. "She won't want a pet that lives that long."

"But it will be sad for her when it dies," Maya said. "It will be sad for all of us, but it will be especially sad for her."

"You're right," Frankie agreed. Maya was always very smart about this sort of thing, which was one of the reasons why Frankie was so grateful to have Maya as a friend. Except that right now they weren't really friends. That thought sank in Frankie's belly like a lead weight. She helped Maya write down all the other information she needed to gather about betta fish: what they ate, what kind of water they needed, that sort of thing.

"Wait. It says there can only be one betta fish in a tank. Otherwise they fight." Maya looked glum. "I really wanted to get two fish at least. I know other people did too. No one's going to vote for just one fish."

Now both Maya and Frankie were glum. Plus, Frankie wasn't sure if they had made up or not. Maya still really wanted a betta fish—Frankie knew that much. And she still wanted a rat—that wasn't going to change. It all made Frankie's stomach twist and gurgle, and she let out a small burp.

"Excuse me," she whispered, but not before Lila looked over and sneered, "Gross!"

"Psst!"

Frankie looked up. It was Ravi. She met him over by the pencil sharpener, grateful for the excuse to get away from Maya and Lila's table. "Ben says he wants a rodent too. He wants a gerbil, but he can be convinced to go for a rat if we give him three chocolate-chip cookies."

"Are you back on Team Rat?" Frankie asked.

"Basically, I just really don't want a fish. I'm playing the odds and think rat has a better chance than a gecko," Ravi replied.

"Where are we going to get three chocolate-chip cookies?" Frankie asked.

Ravi shrugged. "They shouldn't be that hard to procure."

Frankie liked that Ravi used words like "procure," which was basically a fancy word for "get."

"Who else do you think we can get on board?" Frankie asked.

"Can you convince Maya?"

Frankie looked over at Maya, who was studying the computer screen with a furrowed brow. "Maybe," Frankie said, but it was a big maybe. A long shot, really.

"Frankie and Ravi, please get back to your work," Ms. Cupid called to them from across the room. "I'm pretty sure those pencils are sharpened."

"You work on Maya, and I'll try to get Luke. Okay?" Ravi said.

"Okay," Frankie agreed, and hurried back to Maya's table. "Find anything else out?" she asked.

"They come to the surface to gulp air. And the water needs to be warm. They're a tropical fish."

"Sounds hot," Frankie replied. "Listen, I was thinking about what you said about bettas only being able to have one fish in a tank. I think you're right. I mean, one rat would be okay because they're just interesting on their own, but one fish, what would it do? Just swim around?"

"I read that you can actually put a floating mirror in, and then it thinks it's another fish and tries to attack it. It's a way to get exercise."

"Really?" Frankie asked. That actually seemed kind of cool. She wondered if she could make other exercise equipment for a fish. Like maybe a tube for it to swim through. She bet she could make all sorts of cool stuff for a rat. That reminded her that she needed to stay on mission. "Well, so I was thinking maybe the betta isn't a great idea after all."

Maya frowned. "That's what I'm afraid of. But they're so pretty!"

"Pretty isn't everything," Frankie said. "In fact, pretty gets pretty boring, pretty quick."

"Maybe," Maya replied.

"Listen, you've done all this work, so definitely present the betta tomorrow. But maybe when it comes time to vote, since betta fish won't win anyway, you could vote for rat?"

"I don't really like rodents, Frankie. They kind of scare me."

"Scare you? That's ridiculous! There's nothing scary about rodents. Especially not rats. You're just being silly."

"I'm not being silly. Everyone is afraid of something. You're afraid of clowns."

"That's because clowns are scary. But rodents aren't. You just need to spend some time with them. Maybe you could come with me to visit my Aunt Gina at her work. She's got like a hundred rodents. Maybe even a thousand."

Maya shuddered. "No."

"Listen, no one is going to vote for the betta. You shouldn't throw your vote away. Just vote for the rat, okay? If you're really my best friend, you'll do it."

Maya looked like she was considering it, but then Lila leaned over the table. "I've seen a lot of low things, Frankie Sparks, but this takes the cake."

"What do you mean?"

"Trying to convince Maya that her idea is a bad one so that she'll vote for yours instead. I thought you guys were best friends."

That made Frankie's stomach tie itself into a huge knot. Of course she and Maya were best friends. And she was just trying to look out for Maya and be honest, wasn't she?

But then Maya said, "Yeah, Frankie. I thought we were best friends." Frankie's insides slumped to the floor. There was nothing worse than having your best friend think you were no kind of friend at all.

CHAPTER 9

Righting Wrongs

STUPID LILA, FRANKIE THOUGHT AS she walked home with her mom. She kicked at every rock and pinecone that crossed her path. She *was* a good friend. Lila didn't know what she was talking about.

"What's up, kiddo?" her mom asked.

"Nothing," Frankie replied. She kicked another pinecone and sent it shooting out into the road.

"That pinecone might say otherwise."

"Sorry, pinecone," Frankie muttered.

Once they got inside, her mom put two pieces of bread into the toaster. She hummed to herself but didn't say anything. Frankie stewed. And not like the stew that her dad made by dumping a whole bunch of vegetables and potatoes into the slow cooker and letting it warm up all day. No, she was a bubbling-over pot of spicy tomato stew that was splattering all over the kitchen.

Her mom slathered butter all onto the bread, then topped it with sugar and cinnamon. Frankie took her piece and chewed it hard. But it was difficult to stay mad when there was delicious cinnamon-sugar toast in her mouth. So, finally, after not being able to blurt all day, Frankie swallowed her toast and blurted out her problem: "Maya doesn't want a rat for a pet. She wants a fish! A stupid betta fish. She likes it because it's pretty, but really it's boring and it'll die in two years. Plus you can only have one betta fish, so that's extra boring. I was counting on her to vote for a rat, but now Lila told her I was just being mean and trying to get her to vote for something she doesn't even want."

"I'm having a little trouble following all this. I thought your class was deciding what type of rodent to get."

Frankie remembered when she'd first told her mom about the class pet. She guessed she had said it was going to be a rodent. "We're deciding what kind of *pet* to get, and I want a rodent. A rat."

"Okay," her mom said. "So you want a rat and Maya wants a fish, and you think Maya should want a rat?"

"Yes," Frankie replied firmly, but already her

resolve was faltering. Her mom had a way of doing that sometimes. Frankie took another bite of her toast. The sugar stayed on her lips.

"I can see how that might be frustrating for you." Her mom spoke slowly. "Rodents are pretty great."

"They are! And rats are especially great. They are like the octopuses of the land!"

"Amazing!" her mom exclaimed. "What does that mean, precisely?"

"Octopuses and rats are both really, really smart."

Her mom nodded. "You know who else is pretty great? And amazing? And smart?"

Frankie scowled. She knew where this was going. "Maya."

"Maya," her mom agreed. "You guys

have been friends for a long time. And there have been a lot of things you don't agree on. She likes blueberry pancakes, and you like chocolate-chip pancakes. Maya likes stories about girls and horses, and you like nonfiction about science."

"Maya likes her socks to match, and I don't," Frankie added.

"Exactly! And that has never been a problem before. You read your books side by side. Maya gives you her single socks when the matching ones get lost. And Dad lets you each drop blueberries or chocolate chips into your pancakes right on the griddle."

"Or we make our Blueberry Chocolate Flapjacks Extraordinaire," Frankie said.

"Right!"

"But this is different. This time we can't both get what we want."

"Why should Maya have to give up what she wants so that you can have what you want?"

"Because I really, really want it. And Maya only kind of wants a betta fish."

"I see," Frankie's mom replied. Sometimes when her mom said, "I see," it really meant, "You haven't convinced me yet." Frankie's mom pulled off a piece of her toast, put it into her mouth, and chewed carefully. "When one of my programs isn't going the way I want it to, I try to see it from a different perspective." She paused. "Instead of thinking about who wants which pet more, maybe you could think about what matters more to you: having a rat for a class pet or having Maya for a friend."

"I can't compare those two things! That's like comparing whether you want an ice-cream sundae or an all-expenses-paid shark-exploration trip!"

Her mom only raised her eyebrows in reply.

"Oh," Frankie said, realizing the point her mom was trying to make. "But shouldn't she wonder the same thing?"

"She's not asking you to vote for what she wants, right? You guys are friends because of your differences. You've never tried to make her more like you before. I wouldn't start now."

Frankie's mom got up, clearing her plate. "I've got a little more work to do on my

Grabitron project. But if you need to talk more, you know where I am."

"Thanks, Mom."

When Frankie had finished her own snack, she went upstairs. She knew that the first step to solving any problem was research. She looked up betta fish. She had to read a lot of articles, slowly and carefully. But eventually she found what she was looking for: the key to getting back into Maya's heart.

CHAPTER 10

Voting

FRANKIE TRIED TO GET MAYA'S ATTEN-
tion in the playground before school, but Maya
stayed on the swings pumping higher and
higher. Frankie tried again before morning
meeting, but everyone was rushing around.
She tried to sit next to Maya during morning
work, but Ms. Cupid told her to go back to her
own table. She even tried to grab Maya during
snack, but Maya seemed to be avoiding her.

Finally Maya signed out to go to the bathroom. Two friends weren't supposed to leave at the same time, but Frankie decided that this was a moment when rules needed to be broken.

She caught up to Maya right outside the bathroom.

"What is it, Frankie?" Maya asked, her voice sounding sad and tired.

Frankie shook her head. "I need to tell you something about betta fish," Frankie told her.

"Not this again," Maya replied. "I've made up my mind. I want a betta, and I'm not going to vote for a rat."

Maya's words stung, but Frankie had a mission. "Betta fish can be with other fish," Frankie explained. "Just not another betta. The other fish have to be small and not aggressive, but if they don't bother the betta, the betta won't bother them."

Maya hesitated. "Where'd you learn that?"

"I went online last night."

"To find information for me?" Maya asked.

Frankie nodded. "I shouldn't have tried to change your mind. Lila was right, as much as it pains me to admit it."

"Thanks, Frankie!" Maya exclaimed, and threw her arms around her best friend.

Frankie hurried back to class with a big smile on her face. The rest of the class was already on the carpet, ready to begin making their arguments. The principal, Ms. Flower, was there too. She had a notebook and a pen, ready to take down all the information.

Suki raised her hand in her perfectly calm way and got to present first. She wanted fish too, but she wanted these special fish that could glow under a black light. She had even brought in a black light, and she shined it on some fluorescent paper to show how the fish would glow. Ben presented about hermit crabs, which, Frankie had to admit, sounded pretty cool. When a hermit crab outgrew its shell, it crawled out and found a new one. Ben explained how they would need to have a supply of shells on hand, and then they could see which one the hermit crab picked.

Nearly all of the class had presented when Ms. Cupid called on Ravi. He presented about rats before Frankie could, and he shared most of the information she had gathered. Ms. Flower asked, "Does the rat need to be fed every day?"

"I have an answer for that, Ms. Flower," Frankie blurted. "Sorry for calling out."

Frankie lifted up her shoebox and pulled out her invention. "I call it the Automatic Rat Feeder Three Thousand. This is the prototype. Can you hold this a second, Ravi?"

Frankie looped the wire over Ravi's finger and he held the invention above the table. Frankie dug her stuffed mouse out of the box and stood beside Ravi. "See, the rat comes along here. Let's say it's Sunday morning. 'Gee, I'm so hungry!' says the rat." Frankie hopped the stuffed mouse along the table. "'Yum! Food!'" She showed how the rat could just push up on the lever and dump new food into its bowl. "And breakfast is served!" she declared with a flourish.

"Whoa!" exclaimed Luke. "That is way cool."

"Yeah," Suki said. "That is super awesome."

"Rats like fresh pellets. The tube's lid keeps them from getting dried out. And rats are super smart, so it will be easy to train the rat to feed itself."

"Super awesome," Suki said again.

Frankie didn't think Suki had ever thought anything she'd done was awesome, super or otherwise. She couldn't stop beaming. Then

Ms. Flower proclaimed Frankie's invention "very impressive." Frankie thought she might float right up to the ceiling. "It was Ravi's idea too," Frankie explained. "He said we could only have a rodent that could feed itself, so I figured the best thing to do was to make that possible."

"Well, the two of you have made a very strong case for the rat," Ms. Cupid told them. "Nice work." She looked at the clipboard on her lap. "We do have one more presentation. Maya?"

Maya had a stack of index cards, which shook in her hand. Maya hated to be in the front of the room. Frankie gave her a big thumbs-up. A double thumbs-up!

Maya took a deep breath and shared everything she had learned about betta fish. It all came out in one quick stream, but she did it. She took another deep breath and said, "Thanks to Frankie, I know that there can actually be other kinds of fish in the tank. So if we get a betta, we could get another fish too, like maybe the glowing fish Suki talked about, or another small tropical fish."

Maya smiled right at Frankie. Best friends again! Now Frankie thought she might float right up to the atmosphere.

Then the voting slips came out. Frankie looked at her square of paper. She thought about voting for the betta fish as a way of saying she was sorry to Maya. But then she thought about what her mom had told her. The best thing about being friends with Maya was that neither one of them had to change who they were. So, as carefully as she could, Frankie wrote, "Rat."

Each student in the class put their slips into a hat. Ms. Flower opened each slip, and Ms. Cupid made tallies on the whiteboard. "One for rat!" Ms. Flower announced, her voice trilling like a songbird's. She took another slip and carefully unfolded it. Frankie liked Ms. Flower, but she sure could be melodramatic. Frankie wished she would just hurry up.

"Hermit crab!" She pronounced each animal with equal enthusiasm. "Rat!" Frankie's heart sped up. Could it really be happening? "Betta fish! Hermit crab! Glowing fish. Oh! Another glowing fish! And another hermit crab!" On and on it went until there was one more piece of paper. Betta fish had three votes, and glowing fish had five. But hermit crab and rat were tied with six each.

"The last vote wins!" Ben declared.

"Unless it's not a hermit crab or a rat," Suki said. "If it's a glowing fish, then it's a three-way tie!"

"Or it could be the betta fish," Maya suggested. "And then it would still be a rat–hermit crab tie."

Ms. Flower waved the piece of blue paper around. Then she carefully, carefully unfolded it. "The final vote goes to . . ." She let her voice trail off.

"Read it! Read it!" the class started to chant.

Ms. Flower studied the paper. Frankie leaned forward. *Rat! Rat, rat, rat!*

"Hermit crab!" Ms. Flower announced.

Luke hooted and other people clapped. But Frankie felt like a whoopee cushion after it had been sat on. She shriveled down like one too.

hermit crab
Pagurus bernhardus

Someone shriveled down next to her. It was Maya. She held on to Frankie's hand. "I'm sorry, Frankie," she said. "Maybe I should have voted for rat. I guess everyone else thought bettas were boring too."

"Bettas aren't boring," Frankie told her. "I'm sorry I said that. And I'm sorry I asked you to vote for a rat when that really wasn't what you wanted." It was a funny thing about apologizing: Frankie hated doing it, but as she did it, she felt herself puffing up with air. "I'd rather have you as my best friend than a rat."

That made Maya smile, and that made Frankie soar.

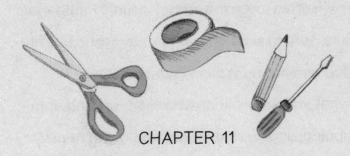

CHAPTER 11

Another Way to Win

FRANKIE WAS THE FIRST ONE TO GET
the classroom job of hermit-crab keeper. At the
end of the day, she made sure Lenny had his
lettuce and his water was full. She tipped the
extra shell so that he could easily climb into
it if by chance he needed a change overnight.
Then she packed up her things and waited for
walkers to be dismissed. Maya walked with
her, since they were having a play date. When

they came down the school stairs, Frankie was surprised to see not only her mom, but also her dad and her aunt Gina waiting.

"Aunt Gina!" she exclaimed, and gave her aunt a big hug. "What are you doing here?"

"No reason," Aunt Gina replied. "Just wanted to see my favorite niece and her best friend in the whole wide world."

"I'm your only niece," Frankie reminded her for the hundredth time.

As they walked home, Frankie and Maya told Aunt Gina all about Lenny.

"He's really cute," Maya cooed. "He pops his head out and looks around like a turtle."

"But he can actually move really fast."

"And he makes little lines in his sand. We

want to teach him how to write messages."

"That would be impressive," Frankie's dad said.

"And entirely impossible," Aunt Gina added. "But good luck to you!"

Frankie and Maya ran up the steps of Frankie's house, through the front door, and straight to the kitchen to get a snack. But Frankie stopped when she saw a big box covered with a blue blanket sitting on the kitchen table. It looked an awful lot like the aquarium covered with fabric that Ms. Cupid had brought into class.

"What's that?" Frankie asked, not daring to hope what might be under that blanket.

"You did a lot of work on your project,

Frankie," her mom explained. "You did a lot of reading and writing, and we know that's not easy for you. We're really proud of you."

"Plus, your invention was quite clever," Aunt Gina said. "In fact I brought it to one of my friends in the library. We have a 3D printer there. He took your prototype and made this!" She whipped the blanket off the box. It was a clear glass aquarium with a multilevel climbing structure inside. It had tubes and slides and ladders, but Frankie could hardly pay attention to it all because there, hanging from the side, was her Automatic Rat Feeder 3000, only instead of being made out of a toilet-paper tube and a yogurt cup, it was made out of bright blue plastic. For the first time ever, one of her prototypes had been made into a real invention!

"I can't believe you made that for me!" Frankie exclaimed.

"That's so cool," Maya agreed.

Then things got even cooler. A small white rat crawled out of one of the tubes.

"Meet our new family member," her mom announced.

Frankie's eyes grew wide. "For real?" she asked.

"For real!" her mom answered.

"What are you going to name her?" Aunt Gina asked. "I'm quite fond of the name 'Gina' myself."

Frankie shook her head. She looked at Maya and smiled. "I'm going to name her Buttercup."

Buttercup wiggled her nose in the air, and so did Frankie. So did Maya. Then Frankie's parents and Aunt Gina joined in too, wiggling their noses in the air like a family of genius rats. Buttercup was right at home!

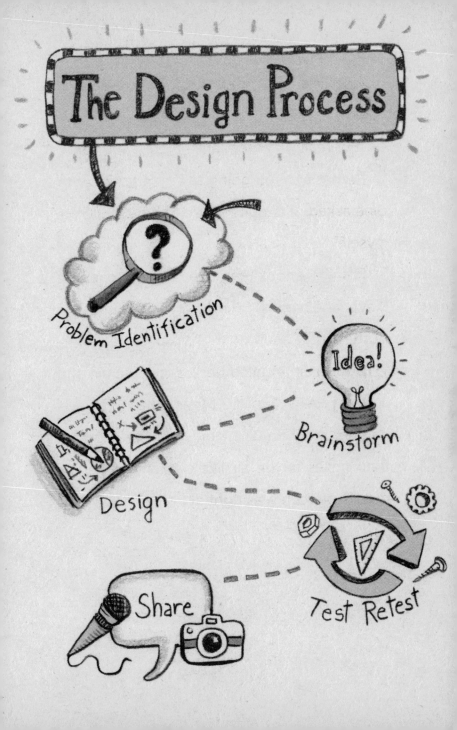

Problems, Problems, Problems

IN THIS STORY FRANKIE HAS A PROB-
lem. She wants a pet rat for the class, but it
needs to be an animal that doesn't need someone to feed it on the weekends.

Before she can start inventing, Frankie
needs to do what engineers call "problem
scoping." You've heard about a microscope,
right? And a telescope? Well, those are tools
that allow us to see things more clearly. When

you problem scope, you're taking a closer look at a problem. You need to find out two things: your expectations and your constraints. These are big words! Basically, the expectations are what you want your invention to be able to do. The constraints are the factors that will limit what you can do. Often constraints are things like time or materials.

Frankie's Expectations:	Frankie's Constraints:
• Rats need new food every day, so the container needs to hold enough food for a weekend. • Rats like their food fresh, not dry, so the container needs to be covered. • The rat needs to be able to feed itself.	**Materials:** Frankie has the materials in her lab. **Time:** Frankie needs to have her invention finished before the class makes their arguments. Frankie needs to be able to make the invention by herself.

Another part of problem scoping is research! Frankie didn't already know everything about rat care, so she had to look up some information in books and online. It was her research that led her to her solution: Because she knew that rats were smart, she knew she could train the class pet to feed itself. Frankie did her research in a few ways:

She read books about rodents.

She talked to an expert: Aunt Gina, the rodentologist.

She used websites that a grown-up (her librarian, Ms. Appleton) recommended.

Your Turn to Be the Inventor!

IMAGINE YOU ARE IN FRANKIE'S CLASS.
What kind of pet would you like to get? Just like Frankie and her friends, you can start by brainstorming a list of possible pets.

Pick one of the animals on your list. Does it meet all the parameters?

1. Fits in aquarium.

2. Costs less than $50.

3. Easily portable.

4. Able to be alone for the weekend—does not need to be fed every day.

If not, what could you design so that it could meet all the parameters and be your class pet?

If you chose a pet that already meets these parameters, can you think of something you could design for the animal to make its habitat more comfortable?

Follow the steps of the design process!

Start by researching a little bit about your animal. You can go to the library to check out nonfiction books or ask a grown-up to help you find good websites online.

Next, brainstorm your invention ideas.

Pick an idea and work on your design. You

can start by sketching, like Frankie did, or look at what materials you have. Remember, you don't need a lot of fancy equipment to build a prototype. You can use recycled materials like cardboard and plastic bottles. If you have toys like LEGO bricks, you can use those, too.

Test your design. How does it work? One of Frankie's attempts would have spilled food all over the rat! She needed to fix that part of her design. Rework your design to fix any problems.

Test again. Keep testing and retesting until you get it just right.

Now share your design with your friends, family, or teacher. They will be excited to see your work!

Acknowledgments

Writing a book is its own special version of the design process, one that is made better through collaboration, so I have many people to thank:

Everyone at Aladdin for jumping on board with Frankie, especially editor Alyson Heller.

Illustrator Nadja Sarell for bringing Frankie to life so vibrantly.

Karen Sherman and Bara MacNeill for catching all the details.

My first reader, Jack Blakemore, who gave me honest feedback.

My character-naming helper, Matilda Blakemore. Frankie literally would not be Frankie without Matilda.

My agent, Sara Crowe, who always finds the best homes for my projects.

My family who supports me every step of the way.

And a very big, special thanks to my students and colleagues at Dyer Elementary in South Portland, Maine. You all inspire me every day!

Don't miss Frankie's next invention!